The Color of Secrets
Encouraging Children to Talk About Abuse

by **Kimberly Steward**
illustrated by **Donovan Foote**

DOGHOUSE PRESS
www.doghousepress.com
PARK FOREST, IL 60466

Doghouse Press
P.O. Box 216
Park Forest, IL 60466
(877) 413-8997
www.doghousepress.com
kimberly@rjsystems.us

Book design and illustrations by Donovan Foote
heysprucemoose@hotmail.com

Edited by Teresa J. Fong-Mei Sit

ISBN: 0-9761497-0-2

Library of Congress Cataloging-in Publication Data
        Steward, Kimberly A., 1947-
                The color of secrets: encouraging children
                to talk about abuse/by Kimberly A. Steward
                p.cm.
                ISBN 0-9761497-0-2

Second Edition October 2005

Dedication

To the healing of children, worldwide, who suffer the secret of abuse.

Appreciation

For his tireless dedication to the incredible illustrations contained in The Color of Secrets, I want to express my appreciation to Donovan Foote. If anyone reading this work would like to contact Donovan, his E-mail is *heysprucemoose@hotmail.com*

For their work in translation to the French and Spanish languages, I offer my utmost thanks to Catherine Aglaure *caglaure@sbcglobal.net*, and Alaina Jasinevicius *lainabean@yahoo.com*, respectively.

I offer my profound thanks to two individuals who have asked to remain anonymous. Your faith in me and support of my work have given me immeasurable joy.

The Color of Secrets

part one

My name is Caroline. I was born into a world filled with color. I live with my Mama, Pa (that's the name we call my daddy), brothers and sisters, and Uncle. We share a secret that makes all of us sad.

I am eight years old. When I was smaller than I am now, I giggled and played with my sisters and brothers. We liked playing on the swings that Pa and Uncle built for us. We also played baseball, jump rope and tag, often laughing as we ran to catch each other. Those were times when life was filled with color, and we kept fun secrets.

Today is my birthday. Not much changes on birthdays because we are poor. Sometimes, when she can, Mama bakes a cake. That won't happen today because Mama said we don't have the money. She gave me a hug and that's just as good - maybe better. When Mama hugs me, little bits of color dance in my head. They make me feel warm inside.

A long time ago, when I was four, something bad happened to me. The bad thing made me sad, so I hid in my dog's house. Her name is Luki. She knew I was sad, because I was hugging her very tightly and crying. She made me feel better by giving me a big doggy kiss on the cheek.

My brothers and sisters think I'm weird because I like to hide. Before Uncle hurt me, I didn't hide as much. But, when the bad thing that happened, kept happening, I started hiding more. I was trying to be invisible. I think they know why. You see, we all keep the same secrets. Big secrets that we have kept since we were little.

The secrets we keep now make me feel scared and unhappy. Sometimes I even feel ashamed or angry. We are glad we have each other to share the secrets with, because talking about them helps us feel better.

I'm a little nervous about telling you the secrets, but I think all children should know that what happened was wrong. Sometimes, after I go to bed, Uncle touches my body in private places. It feels bad and I know he shouldn't touch my privates because he tells me, "It's our secret." If it was okay for him to touch me like that, he wouldn't ask me not to tell anyone.

Sometimes, after he hurts me, Uncle buys things for me, like ice cream or a toy. I hate everything he buys because it makes me think about the bad things he does.

Pa drinks. Mama says he's an alcoholic. When he drinks, he gets really angry. Sometimes he hurts me and my sisters and brothers. I remember the first time very well, because I lost a lot of color that day. Each time he hurts me, I hide more and see less. I think that, if he can't see me, he won't be able to hurt me. I don't like hiding, but it's better than hurting.

I tried telling Pa about Uncle, but Uncle said I lied and Pa believed Uncle. He was very angry and said that I should never lie about Uncle again. He also said that, if I told anyone else, someone would come and take me away, and put me with strangers. He said, "They won't love you like your Mama and I do. You know that, don't you, Caroline?"

I told Pa, "Yes." But I don't think he loves me. I think Mama does, but not Pa. Mama is scared of him too, just like me and my brothers and sisters. I don't believe someone who loved me would hurt me like he does, or ask me to lie about Uncle.

For a long time, the inside of me felt bad. I thought it was my fault that Uncle and Pa hurt me. But a couple of months ago a nice lady came to our school. She talked to us about good touch and bad touch. That was when I knew for sure that Uncle was doing "bad touch" things to me.

Yesterday my teacher told the nurse at my school to look at some marks on my legs. They were from Pa hitting me. The nurse asked me, "How did this happen, Caroline?" I started to cry and told him, "I don't know. I fell." He asked, "Are you sure, Caroline? These marks don't look like you fell." I didn't say anything else.

I heard the nurse say to my teacher, "I'm going to have to report this to the authorities." I got scared when he used that word because I didn't know what it meant. I asked him what it meant and he said, "The authorities are people who care about children who get hurt. They help them feel safe."

I remembered what Pa said and asked him if children always have to go away. He said, "No, Caroline. Sometimes just the person hurting them has to go away, or the parents get help to handle their problems. The most important thing is to make sure that the child doesn't keep getting hurt."

I told him I was afraid I might have to go with strangers who wouldn't like me. He said, "The strangers are people called foster parents. They are people who want to help children who get hurt." He gave me a book to read. It was about foster parents and how they help children who need it. Reading it made me feel better and I decided to trust him.

So, I'm going to give myself a birthday present. When I get to school today, I'm going to talk to the nurse. I'm hoping, after I tell him our secrets, he can help me and my brothers and sisters. I haven't told them. I think they'll try to talk me out of telling. I'll let you know how things turn out.

The Color of Secrets

part Two

The nurse said he was glad I talked to him. He said, "Caroline, it takes a strong person to tell someone about people who are hurting them, especially if you love them." I didn't say anything. I just looked at the floor. Then he said, "Don't be scared, Caroline. You're going to be okay. I'm very proud of you." His words made me feel better.

After he finished talking with me, the nurse made a phone call. I stayed in his office. Sometimes he stopped working for a little while and sat by me. We talked and he gave me some books to read. I liked the books because they had tons of pictures in them.

I know that things won't be easy. After I talked to the nurse, a lady and a man came to my school. They asked me questions about Uncle and Pa. Then, they went to my house. Mama cried when she saw them, but she was happy when the lady helping us said we would be able to stay with her. I was happy, too.

Pa and Uncle had to leave. Uncle can't ever see us again. If Pa visits, he has to come when the lady who helps us can come too. He's getting help for his drinking and, if he gets better, he might be able to live with us again. I hope he gets better. Mama said she misses him, but she's glad he's getting help.

At first my family was angry. Now we agree that I did the best thing. We are all playing baseball again, and jumping rope. We run in the sunshine and play tag. We are learning to giggle again and we already have some new, fun secrets. The color I lost a long time ago is slowly coming back.